River Story

For Michael
M.H.
To Herman, with thanks
B.W.

First published 2000 by Walker Books Ltd
87 Vauxhall Walk, London SE11 5HJ

This edition published 2010

10 9 8 7 6 5 4 3 2 1

Text © 2000 Meredith Hooper
Illustrations © 2000 Bee Willey

The moral rights of the author and illustrator
have been asserted

This book has been typeset in Bembo Educational

Printed in China

British Library Cataloguing in Publication Data:
a catalogue record for this book is available from
the British Library

ISBN 978-1-4063-2593-5

www.walker.co.uk

River Story

Meredith Hooper

illustrated by Bee Willey

WALKER BOOKS
AND SUBSIDIARIES

LONDON · BOSTON · SYDNEY · AUCKLAND

Thousands of rivers help to shape
the surface of our planet. They bring
water and life to the land and all that use it.
Icy-cold racing rivers, slow muddy wide rivers,
long rivers, small rivers, rivers underground.
Each river is different. Each river makes
its own exciting, mysterious journey.

Join us on this one.

All rivers have a beginning…
High in the mountains
the snow is melting.
Trickles of water are running together,

bubbling through moss,
dripping down ledges,
coming together
into a stream.

A small shining stream
slipping over pebbles,

skidding round rocks,
bumping into roots.

Fed by a waterfall,
bouncing down boulders.
Fed by another stream,
smaller and faster.

Snowfalls of water,
springfuls of water,
streamfuls of water,
coming together into a river.

The river races
down deep narrow valleys.
Milky-cold, rattling-bold, fast-moving river.

Scooping up earth,
digging out stones,
mining the mountains,wearing them down.

The river swirls busily
under a bridge.
Stand on the bridge and

look down at the water.
You can't see the bottom.
You can't see how deep.

You can't see the shapes
hidden under the surface.
Trunks of old trees,

16

big fish waiting,
little fish darting,
bottles dropped, treasures lost.

The river is quieter
leaving the mountains.

It winds between meadows,
long strands of waterweed streaking its surface.

19

Willow trees lean their leaves
in the water. People row boats,
trailing their fingers.

Cows come drinking,
their sharp hooves sinking
into the sticky-brown, river-brown mud.

The river grows wider,
and deeper, and stronger.

Fast currents ripple its silky brown surface.
The water moves silently, on to the city.

Inside the city
the river is crowded,
jostled by buildings,
hemmed in by roads.

The traffic moves over
and under and round it.
Drains spill their water,
stray dogs slink by.

And up and down the river go
slow-moving barges and bright busy ferries,

shiny glass tour boats
and tough little tugs.

The river is slowing,
sliding past mudflats,
looping through marshes,

carrying its load of earth and leaves,
tin cans and cartons,
and bits of old wood.

Where the river reaches the edge of the land,
waves wash the sand,
and fresh water meets salt water.

The sea birds are calling.
The sea winds are blowing.
The journey is over.

River journey

All rivers have a beginning and every river has an end.

Go back through the book and match the pictures
to the map, tracing the river from start to finish.
Then turn the page for some good river words.

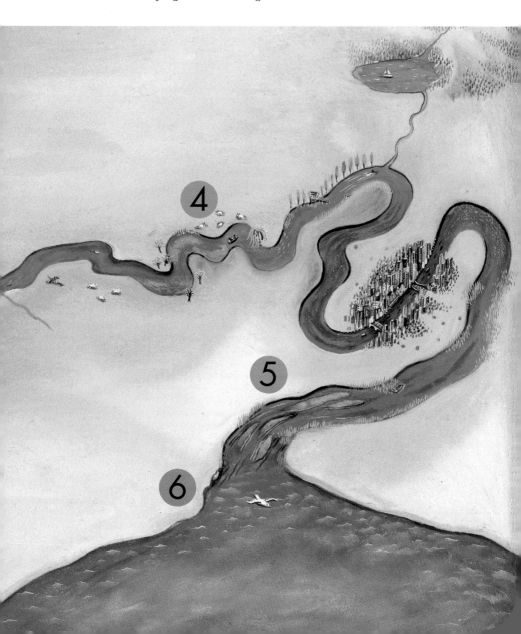

River words

① Source

The beginning of a river is called its source. Some rivers start with melting snow and ice. Others begin with a spring bubbling up from under the ground.

② Tributary

A stream that joins another stream or river is called a tributary.

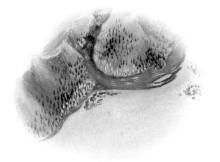

③ Erosion

A fast-moving river carries along lots of pebbles and soil, and these rub against the river bed like sandpaper, slowly wearing it away. This "wearing away" of the land is called erosion.

4 Meanders

A river moves more slowly when it leaves the mountains. Instead of rushing downhill, it often winds around bends called meanders.

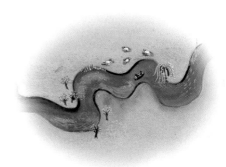

5 Mudflats

A river flows lazily across a flat plain, its muddy water thick with tiny bits of worn rock. Mudflats form where the river dumps this load.

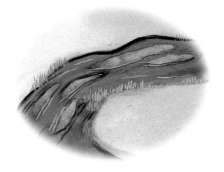

6 River mouth

Sooner or later, all rivers end. They empty their water into lakes, or into the sea.

Index

About the Author

Meredith Hooper has written over
70 books, on everything from pyramids
to aeroplanes to Antarctica. "Growing up
in Australia," she says, "we were taught
to respect rivers, and always take care
near them. That's worth doing,
wherever you are."
This book is based on many rivers
in many parts of the world Meredith
has visited in her travels.

About the Illustrator

Bee Willey has created artwork for books, magazines, even CD covers. With this book, she says, the flow of the river (starting as a trickle, then gaining speed and collecting things on its way to the sea) is like the flow of teamwork that went into making *River Story*. "We had visions, memories and information that we pulled together and turned into a story with a life of its own."

There are 10 titles in the
READ AND DISCOVER series.
Which ones have you read?

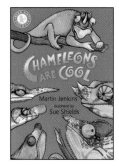

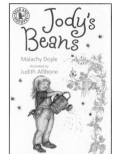

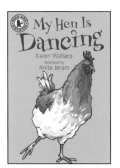
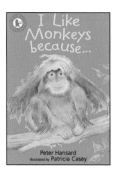
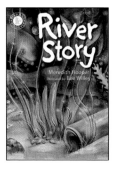

Available from all good booksellers

www.walker.co.uk

FOR THE BEST CHILDREN'S BOOKS, LOOK FOR THE BEAR.